I0547803

I.G. Frederick trades words for cash, specializing in erotic fiction and poetry since 2001. Her erotic short stories appear in Hustler Fantasies, Forum, Foreplay, and Desire Presents, as well as electronic, audio, and print anthologies. Her novels receive high praise from readers, critics, and other authors.

A FemDom, Ms. Frederick, owns the man she adores. Although dominant in the rest of his life, he demonstrates his love by serving as her submissive. Ms. Frederick often writes about finding love in BDSM relationships from the authority of one enjoying that for almost a decade.

http://eroticawriter.net/

Cougar Conquests

**Beautiful older women on the prowl and
the sweet young cubs captured by their allure**

"Benjamin" — A chance meeting at a munch in a tiny town leads Benjamin to an opportunity for training. But, Lady Gina tries to end the relationship rather than emotionally torture herself.

"Festival of Eros" — The handsome young man follows her around all evening, behaving like the perfect submissive ... until she learns his identity.

"Paddles" — A biker bar with no bikers? The decor, name, and patrons of a bar in a small Eastern Oregon town puzzle William who just stopped in for a beer. Then the owner introduces him to the secrets of this very special tavern.

"Starting Over" - When her pet walked out on her, she stayed away from parties because it hurt to watch other women playing with their toys. But, a friend coerces her into attending a unique event.

"The Cougar and the College Boys" — Alone in the woods, hours from Portland, Tess discovers four college friends staying in a nearby cabin. The boys invite her to share their campfire, their dinner, and ...

Cougar Conquests

**Five Sexy Stories
Eight Hot Cubs**

*Beautiful older
women on the
prowl and the
sweet young
cubs captured
by their allure*

I.G. Frederick

Author of Dommemoir & Love Hurts

Cougar Conquests
© 2014 by I.G. Frederick

ISBN: 9781937471101

Pussy Cat Press
http://pussycatpress.com/publisher.html/
P.O. Box 19764
Portland OR 97280

First published electronically in 2012

"Benjamin" first published by *Ravenous Romance*, Jan. 2009
"Paddles" first published by *Forum*, Nov. 2007
"Starting Over" (condensed) published by *Forum*, July 2008

Table of Contents

Benjamin

By I.G. Frederick

I sat at the far end of the munch table, laughing about the latest ordeals that Judith had put her subbie through, when a gorgeous new boy walked in. He had almond-shaped eyes, straight, shoulder-length, black hair, and from what I could see under his knit shirt, a very nice build.

"Hi. Welcome." Dean, the host of our gathering, stood up to greet the stranger. "Are you looking for the munch?"

"Yes I am, thanks." The boy glanced around at the motley crew that gathered weekly to find refuge from our small-town vanilla surroundings. He wiped his hand on his denim-clad thigh before accepting Dean's. "Um, it's my first time."

Duh, I thought. Had to give the boy credit, though, for seeking us out. I'm sure he had enough trouble as one of maybe twenty Asians living in this Eastern Oregon hell hole. He didn't need to add pervert to his credentials. I wondered how long he had waited before finding the nerve to join us. We'd started almost three hours ago. Several folks had left already, and the rest of us would disappear within fifteen minutes.

1

"We're glad you came. I'm Dean. How did you find out about us?" Dean had started the munch five years ago when he moved to this wretched excuse for a place to live. He kept it going through sheer determination.

"I'm Benjamin." Not from a traditional Asian family, apparently, although he could have Americanized his name when he left home. He managed a bit of a smile. Kind of sweet looking. A little younger than I liked, but he might have potential. "You invited me."

Dean laughed. "Collarme.com?"

Benjamin nodded.

"Unfortunately, we're just finishing up." Dean reached for his wallet and laid a couple of tens across the check for his and Sandra's dinners. "Maybe you can come earlier next time."

"Oh, I'm sorry. I thought I read that you started at nine." Benjamin jammed his hands in his pockets.

"No, we end at nine. Start at six. But sit down, I can at least introduce you." Dean pointed at each of us and recited the names of the eleven folks still seated at the table. Although he didn't identify us by orientation, we included four Fem-Doms, five female submissives, and two male Doms.

"How do you identify yourself?" asked Dotty, a smart-ass submissive, which is probably why she's still single.

"I'm not sure, actually. I don't have any experience and have just started to learn about this." Benjamin pulled a chair away from the table and sat with his knees together and hands in his lap.

I leaned over and whispered into Judith's ear. "I'll put money on that boy being a subbie."

"Why would I take that bet?" She rolled her eyes at me. "Do I look like a sucker?" She tossed some bills at her check and stood up. "Got to get home and make sure the boy did all his chores properly."

"Let me know if you need me to come over and help you discipline him." I laughed.

Benjamin's dark eyes widened, but he showed no other reaction. I felt sorry for him. I knew how difficult men found admitting their submissive needs, especially when their culture required them to dominate their relationships. I had to admire the courage he'd shown in venturing to a public forum.

I paid my bill and hugged Judith and Sandra goodbye. Then I sat down next to the new boy. "I'm Lady Gina. Unlike the rest of these folks, I don't have to get up in the morning. Perhaps I can answer some questions for you?"

Benjamin smiled. "Why, thank you so much, Ma'am. Perhaps you'd allow me to purchase you a beverage," he pointed to the table, "since you've already had dinner."

I smiled. "Why don't we go across the street to the pub? I could do with a beer." I walked toward the restaurant exit and Benjamin rushed ahead so he could open the door. At least he had manners, unlike so many of the boys one met online. "How long have you had a profile on Collarme?" I asked when we stepped outside and I saw no one hanging about in listening range.

"Just a few weeks. A friend I met in a chat room told me about it. I've listed myself as a switch, because I don't really know, I mean I'm not sure..."

I laughed. "Why don't you start by telling me what you do know and what interests you about the lifestyle?" I crossed the street in the middle of the block — not like I had to worry about traffic.

"Just what I've seen online. To be honest, I've never met a Domina before."

"You've never met anyone you *knew* was a Domina, perhaps. But I'd be surprised if you'd never encountered one single Dominant woman in your entire life. Have you always lived here?"

"No, Ma'am. I moved here last year to manage the computer systems for the county." Benjamin jumped ahead again to open the door to the pub.

I walked past him. "I prefer the no smoking room." I slowed my pace a little to allow him to catch up and open the door around the corner from the first. Inside, I waited for my eyes to adjust to the darkness, then headed for the back corner. After I slid into the booth, I patted the seat beside me. "Sit here, so we can speak more freely."

He perched on the edge of the seat, as far away as he could balance without falling off.

"I won't bite." I lowered my voice. "At least not until I get to know you better."

Benjamin sucked in his breath. "Yes, Ma'am." He moved over a few inches on the Naugahyde seat. "Thank you."

"I'll have a black butte porter," I told the pretty blonde who appeared to take our order.

"Same," Benjamin added.

I turned and rested my back against the wall and brought one knee up on the bench so I could face my companion while I interrogated him. Before we parted at midnight, I offered him my friendship and agreed to acquaint him with various aspects of the lifestyle.

Benjamin, I found, had an aptitude for all things submissive. I started him out with domestic servitude, teaching him how to clean my house and do my laundry just the way I wanted. Then I introduced him to pain.

The first time I didn't want to overwhelm him, so I just put leather cuffs on the boy's wrists, clipped them to eye hooks on the St. Andrew's cross in my basement dungeon, and gave him a taste of the flogger. I pulled the leather strands across his back, which got him hard, and started with light swats across his butt. Caressing his pretty ass, I enjoyed the heat building there. Then I hit him hard enough to leave marks. He yelped, but his erection never drooped. His eyes glazed over and he flew into subspace. Unfortunately, after only a dozen or so lashes, his virgin skin reddened up, so I reached up to unhook him.

"Please, Mistress, don't stop."

I could barely hear his slurred words. But, I had criss-crossed his back with red streaks. Any more would have raised welts. I dragged my fingernails across the marks.

He moaned, his head dropped, and he hung from his wrists. Unbuckling him from the cross, I helped him over to a chair, and sat down so I could pull him into my arms. He knelt in front of me while I kissed the tears from his cheeks. I let him hide his face against my breasts while I stroked his back, feeling the marks of my whip on his skin.

"Oh, thank you, Mistress." He still whispered, but he enunciated clearly. "That was wonderful."

I waited until he stopped shaking, but then I could no longer restrain myself. The sweetness of the boy, his constant willingness to please me, his enjoyment of my pain, all aroused me. I raised myself off the seat enough to pull off my dripping wet panties, leaned back, and opened my legs. Although I'd only permitted the boy foot worship until now, he didn't hesitate. He kissed the inside of each knee and licked his way up my thighs.

When his nose reached my nether lips, he inhaled deeply. I put one leg behind his neck and pulled him in closer. He drew his tongue slowly across to find my clit. When he flicked my nub in staccato strokes, I shuddered. He wrapped his arms around my legs to prevent me from bucking him off and pushed his face deeper into my moistness. One orgasm led to another until, exhausted, I put my heels on his shoulders and pushed him back.

"Oh, thank you Mistress." He licked off his lips and chin with a besotted grin. "I hope you don't think me impertinent, but that was just delicious."

I laughed. "The pain or me?"

"Well, I enjoyed the pain as well, Mistress, but you taste divine."

I pulled the boy back into my arms and kissed him on the mouth. I could still taste the "divine" juices on his tongue.

I introduced Benjamin to bondage, CBT, single tail, and candle wax. Each visit became more delicious and more painful at the same time. I wanted to fuck him in the ass in the worst way. I wouldn't have minded getting a pussy full of his pretty cock, either. But I considered both of those activities too intimate for someone who would never offer himself to me.

I realized that I needed to end things before I became too emotionally attached. I decided to tell him at his place. That way I could walk away. If he didn't take it well, I wouldn't have to worry about him driving home. I knocked on the door of his small ranch house and it opened. When I stepped inside, I found him standing behind it, naked. As soon as he closed it, he fell to his knees and kissed my feet as I had taught him, finding skin between the leather straps of my sandals. This time, though, I didn't pull his face up to mine. I left him on his knees and walked over to the sofa. He followed on all fours and assumed the position in front of me — ass on his heels, hands palms up on his thighs, back straight, gaze down. For a moment, I just looked at him — so sweet and attractive.

I wish things had turned out differently. He was the first boy in a long time I might have wanted to collar. "I promised to introduce you to the lifestyle and I think you've got enough information now to figure out how to proceed." I took a deep breath. "I know, at the beginning, we talked about remaining friends no matter what you decided you wanted, but unfortunately I can no longer do that."

The boy swallowed.

"You may speak."

"Mistress, I'm sorry if I've displeased you in some way. I

will admit that, at first, I hoped you would decide you might enjoy a friends-with-benefits arrangement, that you would allow me to serve you occasionally. But..." his bottom lip trembled.

I closed my eyes. Looking at him only made this more difficult. "First, I want to assure you that you haven't displeased me in any way. In fact, if you find a woman you wish to present yourself to in hopes of earning her collar, I will provide a reference. But you and I want different things from a D/s relationship. I've grown too fond of you to continue what essentially will become training for another woman." My voice cracked. Needing to leave before I burst into tears, I rose and headed for the door. "I wish you the best. You may keep in touch by e-mail, if you want, and let me know if you find your One." I had my hand on the doorknob when I heard him scurrying up behind me.

"I beg you, Mistress, don't go. Please, let me speak." He prostrated himself in front of the door, his chest on the tile floor, his cheek against my feet.

I blinked rapidly.

"Please, may I speak, Mistress." He covered my toes with kisses.

I nodded, realized he couldn't see that and whispered, "Yes."

"Mistress, you're correct, of course. I enjoy service. Ideally I would find someone who might accept that from me part time. I know that's not enough for you. I also know I love you. No, I adore you. I only want to spend whatever time you'll allow me at your feet. If to do that, I need to forfeit my freedom and give myself to you as your twenty-four/seven slave ... well, I'd much rather do that than live without you."

I gripped the doorknob harder for support. To keep my legs from shaking, I leaned my forehead against the painted wood.

"I'm begging you, Mistress. Will you please train me to be your perfect slave so I can devote my life to pleasing you?"

I put one hand over my mouth to stifle a sob and took two deep breaths before reaching down to grab his thick hair and pull him up onto his knees. I leaned over and kissed him, pressing my lips hard against his, thrusting my tongue deep into his mouth. He sucked on it eagerly, but kept his hands by his side as I had taught him. I released his hair and lifted his arms upward until he got my message and reached behind me. He slid his hands up my calves and thighs to wrap his arms around my ass. I had one hand tangled in his hair, holding his head back, and the other pressed against his cheek. *Damn, I don't even have a strap-on with me.*

I finally released the boy and stood upright. "Are you sure? You realize if you decide to give yourself to me, that's the last decision you'll ever make."

"Yes, Mistress."

"You're willing to be kept in chastity, sign a power of attorney, turn your home and your bank account over to me?"

His face paled and I could see his Adam's apple working. "Yes, Mistress."

I kissed him again. I knew we'd need to repeat this discussion when he wasn't distraught. But I'd never expected him to give himself to me. That he'd even consider doing so, magnified my desire for him. I could take him under consideration, and put a training collar on him so he could experience what slavery truly meant. Then we could both find out if he really did love me that much. I grabbed his hair and dragged him behind me toward the bedroom.

"Mistress, may I get something you might wish to use in there?"

Surprised, I released him. He scurried over to the kitchen table, retrieved a box wrapped in gold paper and tied with royal blue ribbons, and scuttled back. He knelt in front of me, offering the box. "You mentioned, once, that you wanted one of these. I hope purchasing it for you wasn't out of line."

I took the box with one hand, his hair with the other, and continued to the bedroom. There, I sat on the bed and ripped away the paper while lifting my feet towards the boy's face so he would remove my sandals and kiss my toes. Inside the box, I found a double-sided dildo — the kind you can use without a harness, one end bent at an angle with a nice thick bulb for stimulating me while I fucked him. The box also contained a bottle of lube.

I pushed myself back on the bed and let the boy kiss his way up my legs to my crotch. I raised my hips so he could ease off my shorts and panties. Between the allure of owning this boy, the thoughtfulness of his gift, and the adoration with which he licked the inside of my thighs, I was so turned on that I came the minute his tongue touched my clit.

I let him bring me off several times before I grabbed his hair and pulled his face up to mine. I kissed him and rolled him over on his back. While he watched, I coated the larger end of the dildo with lube. Then I slipped the bulb end inside me. He spread his legs and I placed the lubed end against his asshole. When I eased it in slowly, he sucked in his breath. Holding it in place with one hand, I propped myself up with the other, watching with delight as the boy gave in to the pleasure of the moment. I lay my body across his and kissed him, sucking on his tongue, biting his lip, his hard cock pressed against my belly. The base of the shaft rubbed against my clit and I shuddered with another orgasm.

I paused, panting, and pushed the boy's fingers toward the buttons of my blouse. With a reverent look in his eyes, he unfastened it and slipped it off my arms. He reached for my bra hooks, looking a question. When I nodded, he undid them and caressed my tits. I moved inside him until I came again.

Slowly I eased the dildo out of his ass and he whimpered. It came out of my pussy with a sucking noise making me laugh. He smiled at me and I crawled up far enough to stick a tit in his mouth. He closed his eyes and teased my nipple with his tongue until I slid back down and grabbed his cock. I squeezed it hard enough to hurt and the look of painful pleasure on his face just made me want more. I guided it in and then grabbed his balls, twisting them until he cried out in pain. While I moved up and down, I leaned over and alternated biting his nipples and raking my fingernails across his chest. When I gave the boy permission, he came with a shout, clutching at my ass, thrusting up into me hard enough to bring me off again.

I let him stay there until he softened and slid out of me. Then I rolled over on my back and made him lick me clean. When I couldn't stand to come one more time, I grabbed his hair and pulled him up so I could hold him in my arms. I lay there for half an hour, floating in the euphoria, throbbing from countless orgasms. I thought how wonderful his service would make my life. But I couldn't forget that he hadn't sought a Mistress/slave relationship.

"What will you tell your family?" Another issue to consider.

He blinked and shook his head a little."They don't have to know. I almost never see them, anyway."

"Do you understand the consequences of living in a mixed-race relationship in a small town?"

"A company I used to work for contacted me about moving back to Portland. I didn't consider it because I didn't want to leave you." He pressed his lips against my neck for a moment.

Well, that would eliminate some of the mixed couple issues. And his family lived in Spokane, so we'd have more distance between us. "I'd welcome the opportunity to get out of this hell hole. I could never afford to move on my own." If he decided he really couldn't accept life as a twenty-four/seven slave, at least in Portland I'd have a better chance of meeting someone who could.

"The company would pay for the move. I'd earn enough to support you, you wouldn't have to worry about finding a job."

"I suppose, between our two houses, we'd have enough

for a down payment there." I ran my fingers through the silky strands of his hair.

"Whatever you wish, Mistress. The only thing that matters to me is the privilege and honor of serving you — however, whenever, whatever way you want."

I grabbed the boy's hair and pulled his head back so I could look in those exotic eyes. Anything but inscrutable, they stared back at me with the adoration I craved. "I have no ties here, boy." I kissed him. "I planned on walking away from you tonight because spending time with you, thinking you'd never give yourself to me, had become too painful. Owning you will make me incredibly happy."

He smiled. "Which is all I ever want to do."

Festival of Eros

By I.G. Frederick

"Did you send him that same wretched picture from the trip to the mountain when you looked like death warmed over?"

Sylvie crossed one slender leg over the other. "Only photo I have that jerk ass isn't in."

Martha shook her head and stirred the mud-colored mixture in her giant yellow cup. "You could let someone take a better picture."

Sipping unadulterated coffee, Sylvie shrugged. "Really, if someone stops writing because he doesn't like my photo, I don't think I'm missing out on much. That kinda guy's gonna disappear when my hair turns grey and I gain a few pounds." She twirled long, black tresses around one finger.

"At the rate you're going, you'll *be* grey and weigh a hundred and fifty pounds before you'll meet anyone."

Sylvie shuddered at the thought of carrying that much weight around on her five-foot frame. She worked hard at keeping fit and was proud that at forty-five she still didn't

13

need to color her hair. But, although the thirty-two-year-old Joshua had seemed very attractive when they corresponded, his insistence on a photo, and his silence since she sent one, had made him easy to forget. "Why are you so eager to see me fixed up anyway? Robert only moved back to Virginia six months ago."

"Because I'm tired of listening to you whine about how you don't have anyone to serve you and none of the boys at the FemDom events know how to worship your feet properly."

"What are you wearing tonight?" Sylvie emptied her cup.

Martha looked at her over the rims of her black-plastic-framed glasses. "Don't think I don't know you're trying to change the subject. Besides, I hadn't really thought about it that much. I'm not sure I'm going if Brad can't make it."

"Hey, girlfriend. I don't care if you bring your subbie along, but don't desert me if he gets stuck at work. I've looked forward to the Festival of Eros for almost a month now."

"You *could* go by yourself. You'll know more than half of the folks attending."

"Don't want to go by myself. I get too depressed, especially when I see other women there with their boys on leash." Sylvia pulled the strand of hair into her mouth and chewed on it. Although Robert had returned to Virginia to care for his ailing mother, he had asked her to remove his collar before he left, severing all hope that they could continue their relationship long distance or after his mother died.

Martha sighed. "You know, for a FemDom, you can be damned submissive."

Sylvie scowled. "Not submissive. Just lonely."

Without a boy to help her get dressed, and knowing with Brad working Martha felt put upon just going with her, Sylvie didn't even try to get into a corset. Instead she wiggled into a strapless, skin-tight, silky black dress. It hugged her slender figure, emphasizing the swell of her breasts and setting off her pale creamy skin. She chose a pair of long, dangling gold chain earrings that slid across her bare shoulders and added a gold bracelet watch. It needed a battery and didn't tell time, but it emphasized her tiny wrist. Three-inch, spiked, patent-leather heals completed her outfit.

She turned in front of the full-length mirror on the back of her bathroom door and wondered why she bothered. She knew most of the submissive males in the greater metropolitan area. The ones she found attractive were either already taken or couldn't believe such a tiny thing could dominate them. She reached for her cell to tell Martha to forget about it, when the doorbell rang.

"Well, at least you dressed up for the occasion," Martha said when Sylvie opened the door. Martha wore a red latex dress that emphasized her ample bosom and hips. Even though her skin was covered from neck to below the knee, she resonated sex appeal.

When they arrived at the center, Sylvie could almost hear the whiplash as heads snapped around to stare at them. She smiled and handed her ticket to the fellow in a black taffeta maid's outfit, allowing him to encircle her right wrist with a paper band. "Ma'am, my shift ends in an hour if you'd like someone to show you around?" He curtsied.

"Thanks, but my girl and I have plans." They didn't, but Sylvie had no interest in men who couldn't submit unless they dressed up in women's clothing.

Once they stepped inside the second set of doors, the music enveloped them in a rhythm that made Sylvie want to find the dance floor. Industrial rock blared from speakers at the far end of the room. They were almost as tall as she. Before she could look further, she did a whiplash of her own. To the right of the entrance, an Asian man was layering vegetables in patterns on a naked woman posed on a massage table. Sylvie stared, mesmerized. When he completed his masterpiece and photographed his work, he removed the food and invited Sylvie to volunteer. She shook her head, but the woman next to her dove for the table and became a fruit platter.

Martha tugged her sleeve and they wandered by the paintings, photographs, and sculptures of nude and partially clothed bodies entangled in ways even Sylvie hadn't imagined. They stopped to watch a woman wearing only a thong get painted in purple, black, and blue body paints then stand on a platform posed like a statue.

When they reached the main stage, an ensemble wove in and out of complex patterns fascinating to watch. But the performance only made Sylvie want to dance even more. She tugged at Martha's arm and pointed to the dance floor now visible in the back of the cavernous hall. Martha grimaced, but followed Sylvie through the crowd standing in front of the stage.

As soon as they reached the edge of the undulating bodies, Sylvie broke out into a sultry dance that didn't quite fit the speed of the music, but she made it work. Lost in the beat, in the caress of silk against her skin, in the sensual movement of her muscles, she jumped when two fingers tapped her shoulder. She opened her eyes to find a six-foot tall, blue-eyed, blond hunk looking down at her.

"May I have a dance?"

He wore tight black leather pants, a leather vest that exposed a muscular, almost hairless chest, and powerful arms with a dragon tattoo that extended from his right bicep across his shoulder. *Probably Dom*, Sylvie thought to herself. *But, he just wants to dance.*

She looked at Martha who grinned from ear to ear and nodded. Sylvie frowned. It was just a dance. The song ended and the DJ did a one-eighty, playing Pink's "Fucking Perfect." The man held his arms opened and Sylvie hesitated for a moment before stepping into them. He held her lightly and she let him lead. The beat increased but the DJ stuck with Pink's mellower songs. It seemed incongruous and Sylvie wondered at his choices, but given that she had a gorgeous young man who smelled of leather and spearmint to twirl around the dance floor with, asking too many questions didn't seem wise.

After their third dance, the DJ announced that a comedy act would take the main stage and he would return with more music once it was done. Sylvie stepped back and smiled up at the stranger. "Thanks, that was fun." She turned around to look for Martha.

He leaned down and whispered. "May I buy you a drink?" When she didn't answer right away, he said. "I promise I won't bite, unless you ask me to."

Sylvie turned around and she knew one eyebrow had crept above the other. "Thanks for the dances, but I prefer to do the biting."

Before she could turn away, he dropped to one knee. "I switch."

Sylvie blinked rapidly, not believing what she saw. She grinned. "In that case," she pointed to café tables set up far enough from the speakers that one might have a conversation, "I'll be over there. You may bring me a glass of red wine."

"Yes, Ma'am. Thank you, Ma'am." He bowed his head before rising and striding toward the bar behind the main stage.

For a moment, Sylvie watched his fine ass, thinking how lovely it would be to mark with her whip. She turned toward the tables and chose one near the black curtains that hid the cinder block walls and softened the hall's normally austere interior. He set a glass of wine in front of her and stood, holding a Widmer bottle, next to the chair opposite until she nodded permission for him to sit down.

Trained. She smiled again and took a sip, enjoying flavors of berries and cherries combined with subtle nuances of mocha and spice.

"I have a confession to make."

"We just met, what is it you feel the need to confess?"

"I bribed the DJ to play slower music so I could dance arm in arm with you instead of just watching the amazing way you move."

Sylvie looked at him, puzzled.

His eye held a glint of mischief. "I saw you staring at the body painting and I wanted more than anything to approach you. But, you kept moving and I wasn't sure if you and the woman you came in with were a couple until I saw you dancing."

She tilted her head.

"I can always tell the difference between two women who have just gone out on the dance floor together and two women who are dancing together." He smiled revealing even white teeth. "The DJ's a friend of mine and he owes me some money so I told him I'd forgive his debt if he would play something more conducive to ..." He reached forward and lifted her fingers to his lips, just grazing them but leaving them warm and tingly "... contact dancing."

Sylvie beamed. She had enjoyed dancing with him and couldn't help but think what it might be like to kiss him and bite those lips.

The more she talked with him, the more appealing he seemed. But, she'd looked forward to this show for months and didn't want to miss anything. When she finished her wine, she rose to her feet. "I want to see the rest of the exhibits."

"If Ma'am would permit it, I would be most honored to accompany her."

Sylvie only nodded, but the tingle in her hands was creeping across her torso. *Stop it.* She mentally slapped herself. *You just met and for all you know he owns a sub and is just toying with you.* More than one Dominant male had tried, always very unsuccessfully, to convince her that she really wanted to bottom, but just hadn't yet met the right man.

Sylvie wandered the exhibits. The stranger followed respectfully, always a few feet behind her. Whenever she turned to comment on a photograph, or ask him whatever question had popped into her mind, he stepped forward just enough so he could lean down where she could hear him over the techno music once again blaring over the speakers.

"Sylvie!" Belinda embraced her in a hug almost before Sylvie saw her come around the corner with Bennie in tow. "How are you darling? Who's your new boy?"

Sylvie shook her head, but Belinda reached around her to shake the stranger's hand. "Hi, I'm Ms. B. I run the FemDom teas at the Viper. How come we've never seen you there?"

"I'm not much for serving just any woman. She has to be the right one."

Sylvie wondered if looks were his primary motivation. Some of the women who attended the teas were a bit old and frumpy, although others made her seem plain in comparison.

"I see." Belinda squared her shoulders. She was a bit of a female supremist and believed all males should bow before all women. "Well, you've picked a winner in our Sylvie: smart, gorgeous, and as dominant as they come."

Sylvie stopped herself from rolling her eyes. "I've still quite a bit of the exhibit left to see, dear. We can catch up at the next tea. Nice seeing you, Bennie." She nodded at the boy who bowed from the waist.

"Of course, dear." Belinda gave her a hug. "You'll have to bring your pretty toy."

Sylvie refrained from telling Belinda he wasn't hers, as much from protecting him as from her own desire to see the rest of the art. In the next section, a crowd had gathered to watch Dick tying two almost-naked women together while one stood on her hands.

Edging around the crowd, Sylvie ran into Rupert who wore a floor-length sleeveless silk sheath, with elbow length opera gloves. "Good evening, Ma'am." The look he gave the stranger, who stepped just a little closer, definitely had a green cast. "I hope you're enjoying yourself."

"I am, dear, thank you. You look lovely tonight."

Rupert batted his false eyelashes and pulled up his gloves. "Oh, thank you, Ma'am. Coming from you that means so much."

"Didn't you want to catch the next show, Ma'am." The voice in her ear had become familiar. But the deep sexy timbre still made her quiver inside.

"Thanks for reminding me." She smiled at Rupert. "I'm sure I'll see you later."

Sylvie headed for the stage area. "What is the next show?"

He shrugged. "No clue. Just sensed you'd like extraction from that encounter. I take it you're not fond of sissy boys?"

"Just not my type."

"And, may I ask, Ma'am, what is your type?"

I'm guessing we both already know the answer to that. Sylvie allowed herself to be distracted by a display of pony art. The last photograph showed a petite woman in leather riding a saddled male. Although he stood upright, he wore a butt plug tail, blinders, a bridle with a bit, a metal chastity device, and nothing else. Sylvie sighed.

"I would be honored to carry Ma'am on my back that way. Do you know where I might purchase the necessary equipment?"

She turned and looked up at him. He wasn't kidding. "I'm sure I can find out."

"The performance art here has been decidedly oriented toward male tops. Perhaps something like that," he nodded toward the painting, "would be a welcome addition next year."

The man sure knows how to win a Domme's interest.

"Hey, Sylvie, how ya doing?" Burt approached from her blind side, but she recognized his voice. He was one of those men who had tried to convince her she should be a sub. Of course, even if he'd offered to serve her, she would have turned him down. He was at least sixty pounds overweight and hairy as a bear except on his head which was almost bald.

"Fine, thanks. And you." She backed away from the smell of alcohol and cigarettes.

The stranger stepped in front of her. "Nice to meet you, Burt. What do you think of all this?" He waved his hand so that his arm intercepted Burt's view of Sylvie and she slipped around a corner.

He found her admiring a beautiful marble sculpture of two naked men embracing. She looked up at him. "You're good."

"With the right woman."

"And, what makes you think I'm the right woman?" She drew quote marks in the air with her fingers.

"To be honest, Ma'am, I don't know. I admit you're gorgeous and I find you incredibly attractive. But there's more to it than that. You bring out a desire to prostate myself at your feet."

Her toe twitched at the thought.

"Speaking of which, Ma'am's been walking around for hours in those heels. Perhaps she would like a foot massage as a way of testing my talents?"

Her feet did ache and Sylvie could think of nothing more appealing at the moment. She pointed to an empty sofa in one of the alcoves off to the side. "I'll be there. Bring me some cold water."

"Oh, yes, Ma'am. Thank you, Ma'am."

The alcove had been designed to resemble a living room with carpeted floor and pillows scattered about. She propped several against the back of the sofa so she could lean against something and her feet would still reach the floor. He arrived moments after she settled herself, put a bottle of water on the small table near her hand, and dropped to his knees. She lifted one foot and he slipped off her shoe.

While massaging the ball of her foot with his thumbs, he kissed her toes one by one. Sylvie melted into the pillows. His lips glided slowly toward her ankle while his thumbs kneaded all the pain from her toes to her heel. She sighed — it had been so long. He reversed directions and she had to clench her muscles to avoid wriggling in delight. She wondered if he could smell her arousal. At that moment, he looked up at her and she knew the answer by the twinkle in his eye. But then, he couldn't hide much in his tight leather pants and he was obviously just as turned on as she was.

He kissed her pulse point on the inside of her ankle, slipped her shoe back on, and reached for her other foot, repeating his ministrations and sending Sylvie into an ecstatic bliss. The heat of his lips on her bare skin made her grateful she'd chosen not to wear hose. Lost in the sensual assault on her skin and muscles, in the aphrodisiac of having a tall, strong man kneel before her, Sylvie floated in euphoria. As her arousal swelled to encompass every part of her body, she couldn't help wonder what his tongue would feel like between her legs. That thought pushed her over the edge and she shuddered. The stranger chuckled. When she was finally able to open her eyes, he looked very pleased with himself.

He gently lifted both her feet onto the sofa and rested his head on her hand. She managed to extract it, leaving his head resting on her hip, so she could stroke his shoulder-length, silky, blond hair. She couldn't resist grabbing a handful and pulling his head back so she could look into his eyes. *Wow*, she thought when she saw the ardor intensifying the blue.

She pulled his face to hers and kissed him, exploring his lips with her tongue. Grabbing his bottom lip with her teeth, she pressed down just enough to test his reaction. He moaned.

Not here. Although no one would object in this venue, if she got more intimate with the boy, they would attract an audience. Sylvie wasn't that much of an exhibitionist. She pulled away and released his hair.

He kissed her fingers. "If Ma'am is pleased with my service, perhaps she would consider giving me her telephone number or e-mail address so I may contact her about serving her again? Perhaps in a more private setting?"

Sylvie fumbled in her handbag and extracted one of the

calling cards which only had her scene name and an e-mail address. The stranger gasped.

"Lady Sensual?" He lifted his head. "I'm Joshua."

Sylvie felt one eyebrow creep above the other again. What a downer way to end a lovely evening.

"Oh, Ma'am, I'm so sorry." He pressed his lips to the back of her hand. "When you get home, you'll find several e-mails from me. I only this afternoon discovered that for some reason your last three messages to me ended up in my spam folder. I'd just thought you found my photograph unappealing and that you stopped writing. I was traveling, so I was distracted and didn't follow up."

Sylvie had to laugh. He looked so adorable, on his knees, pleading with his eyes. She thought about all the wonderful things that Joshua had promised to do for her and the lovely way he had worshiped her feet. "I still have your phone number in my e-mail somewhere. I will call you tomorrow and we can discuss how and when you will serve me."

She swung her feet off the sofa and took a long swig from the now warm water in the bottle. He extended his hand and she used it to steady herself as she rose to her feet. "But, right now I want to dance with you some more."

Paddles

By I.G. Frederick

I leaned my Hog on the kickstand, batted at my leathers to knock off some of the road dust, and entered the tavern. Paddles seemed like a strange name for a watering hole in a town three blocks long, but I thought Kallum, Oregon, might have a factory that made ping pong paddles, or maybe fan blades.

I caught the door with my back and blinked until my eyes adjusted to the dim interior. Paddles looked like any small-town bar — a few round tables surrounded by ladder-backed chairs, stained and dented bar painted black with black, vinyl-topped chrome stools. Behind the bar, a mirror filled the width of the wall with neon signs for various beer brands above it. In the middle of those hung a pair of small oars, with truncated handles, crossed over each other, but I didn't see any other nautical decor.

I noticed half a dozen men who also wore leathers at one end of the bar, although I hadn't seen any other bikes out front. Perhaps the place had a parking lot in back that I hadn't noticed.

I wandered over to the opposite end of the bar and swung one hip onto the bar stool. The bartender, a plump blonde, wore a tight black top that pushed her tits up in luscious mounds under her chin. She had a black rose on a thorny stem tattooed on the left one. Without moving from the spot where she leaned on the bar talking to the other folks, she called out: "Whatcha drinking, boy?"

I didn't think she looked more than ten years older than me, so I'm not sure what she meant by that, but I needed a beer so I asked: "What have you got on tap?"

"Can you read, boy?" She lifted one hand and pointed a long fingernail, painted black, at a chalkboard, barely visible in the dim light, next to the neon Widmer sign.

"Sorry, didn't see the board, Ma'am." I figured if she wanted to call me boy, I'd at least stay respectful. "Could I have a Hefeweizen?"

In one fluid movement, she pushed herself off the bar, grabbed a glass mug, and turned to the taps that lined the back wall under the mirror. She set the full mug on a round, paperboard coaster in front of me. "Four-fifty."

"Thank you, Ma'am." I dug a fiver out of my pocket and set it on the bar. "Keep the change."

She smiled, painted red lips parting to reveal white teeth. For some reason, the idea of those teeth biting my nipple planted itself in my brain and raised a boner. *Where the hell did that come from*, I wondered.

"Whatchyername, boy?" She tapped a black lacquered fingernail on the bar.

"William, Ma'am. And yours?" The beer had a strong, yeasty flavor.

"Boys 'round here just call me Mistress." She grinned again and I saw a wicked glint in her eyes. "But you're not from 'round here, are you, boy?"

"No, Ma'am. Just passing through." Her dark eyes stared right through me as if she could see through my leathers and knew exactly how hard I had gotten. "Riding my bike from

Portland to Boise to visit my family." I thought I'd volunteered enough information, but she continued to stare. "Just thought I'd stop for a brew to wash away the road dust. Didn't know this was a biker bar."

Her wicked laugh grabbed me by the balls. "A biker bar! Whatever gave you that idea, boy?"

I nodded my head toward the fellows wearing leather chaps and vests who had moved from the bar to a table.

She laughed again, louder and longer this time. With a gaze that could have lit coals, she studied me from head to toe. "I'm guessin' you don't have any experience." She licked her lips. "But, I bet you're a natural."

"Natural what?"

"Mistress, could we please have another round over here," one of the leather clad fellows called out.

"You need to get to Boise by a certain time?" She reached for a pitcher and held it under one of the taps.

"No, Ma'am. I thought I'd take my time, enjoy the ride."

"Maybe you should plan on staying here in Kallum for a day or two. I could teach you a few things." She winked and her smile reminded me of a cat watching a mouse. When she carried the pitcher around the end of the bar, her hips swayed provocatively. I had to admit, if she meant her statement as an invitation, I'd find it hard to resist her ample ass and big bazookas. I downed the rest of my beer in one long swallow.

When I set the glass down on the bar, a second board, on the other side of the mirror, caught my eye. In red chalk it touted a chili and cornbread special. When the bartender came back to stand in front of me, I pushed my glass towards her. "I'll take another, please, and I'll have the chili special."

"Cup or bowl?"

"Whichever's bigger."

She set my refilled mug back on the coaster and raised one perfectly arched eyebrow. "Shall I start a tab?"

I smiled. "Sure, guess I'll stick around for a bit."

"You belong to anyone?"

I pondered her meaning. "I'm not currently involved, no." I flushed a little. My last girlfriend had stomped out after calling me the wimpiest biker she'd ever known. Guess only wimps treat woman with respect these days.

The bartender got that wicked glint in her eyes again. She sashayed down to the other end of the bar, ladled something from a big black kettle into a bowl, opened a warming drawer, and brought me the large bowl, a plate with a huge hunk of cornbread, and tableware wrapped in a paper napkin.

I unrolled the napkin, spread it out over one thigh, and dipped the spoon into chunks of meat swimming in a stew of beans and onions. The spoon steamed when I brought it to my mouth so I blew on it. The scent of chili pepper wafted back at me. By the time I emptied the bowl, my mouth burned. I had finished my second beer and started on a third.

"Enjoy?" The bartender removed the empty bowl and plate, sliding them into a tub under the bar.

"Yes, Ma'am. Quite tasty." I swallowed the rest of my beer to quench the fire in my mouth.

"I can make you forget that discomfort." She picked up some kind of remote control device with a short antenna from the counter under the mirror and pressed the top button.

I heard stomping on stairs and a red-headed kid wearing only a black Speedo and a leather collar around his neck charged into the bar and fell on his knees in front of the bartender. He had to have a cup on or some such, because the bulge at his crotch had an odd shape. Kid didn't look old enough to serve beer never mind drink it.

"I'm going to take this boy downstairs and give him a taste." She patted the kid on the head. "You mind the bar."

"Yes, Mistress. Thank you, Mistress." The kid had red welts across his back and I wondered if he'd fallen backwards into blackberry brambles.

The bartender came around the bar and took my hand. She pulled me off the stool and led me to a door at the opposite end of the bar.

"Ma'am, do you mind if I use the restroom first?"

She nodded and leaned against the wall while I pulled open the men's room door, next to the one she had headed for. When I stepped out again, she stood near the table with the other bikers laughing. She leaned down and said something I couldn't hear, then came back. I followed her down rickety wooden steps lit by a single bulb.

An X-shaped cross leaned against one wall and shackles hung from chains attached to the cement walls. A metal cage filled one corner, with a padded table that bristled with eyebolts, and a weird looking chair thing standing next to it. My breath caught in my throat. "Ma'am," I managed to get out between suddenly parched lips. "I think you may have misunderstood my interest."

She grabbed my wrist, twisted my hand up behind my back and pulled until she forced me to my knees on the hard cement. "Your interests are irrelevant." With her other hand, she grabbed a handful of my hair, pulled my head back and kissed me on the mouth. I tried to pull away, but any movement tugged on my hair and hurt. Besides, I couldn't ignore my reaction to her kiss. She thrust her tongue deep into my mouth and I got hard enough to make my jeans uncomfortable.

She released me. "Strip, boy."

I just stared at her, but my fingers unbuttoned my shirt while I did. When I had removed it and my leather vest, she stepped close again and ran her fingers across my shoulders. She buckled a leather collar around my neck. "Continue."

"May I stand to remove my pants?"

She grinned like a cat who had gotten in the cream. "Knew you were a natural. You may address me as Mistress, boy."

"Yes, Ma'am. May I stand, Mistress."

"Yes."

I rose to my feet, unbuckled my leathers and undid the button and zipper of my jeans. Leaning against a metal post supporting the ceiling, I pulled off my boots. Then I tugged the ankles of my jeans and chaps, pulling them off together.

"Very nice." She ran one hand along my naked ass and my cock got harder. "Mmmm." She stroked the underside and my rod jumped up at her.

With her left hand, she grabbed it and tugged. Of course, I followed. She led me over to the chair thing and made me kneel on the padded leather seat. She pulled me over the leather back so my ass stuck up and my head hung down. Then she fastened leather cuffs around my wrists and ankles and clipped them to eyebolts sticking out of the wooden parts with snap rings. I couldn't believe I had allowed this woman to bind me. Before, I could have overpowered her and left. Now, I had no choice but to endure whatever perversions she chose to inflict. Still, I had to admit the thought of her having complete control over me proved such a turn on my balls ached. She seemed to know what she was doing, so I decided to go with the flow.

I felt strips of leather caress my back. Then I heard the leather whistling through the air and those strips landed all at the same time across my backside. I yelped in surprise, but although she hit hard, the pain sent a thrill down to my swollen cock. She kept swatting me with her leather strips, occasionally pausing to run a hand across my smarting ass. Once she even grabbed my balls and twisted my sack. As much as that hurt, it still increased the ache in my cock. I longed for some form of release.

She must have gotten rid of the leather because she stroked my sore cheeks with both hands. Her cool palms felt good against the welts she'd raised and I wiggled my ass a little. That brought a reaction I hadn't expected. She hit me again, but this time with a wide, smooth wooden paddle. Where the leather stung, this generated a thudding pain. I hung over the back of the chair, my ass sore, my cock hard, wondering how I'd gotten myself into this predicament.

Then she pressed herself against me and I realized she'd removed her own clothing. Her firm tits pushed against my back and I wanted to reach around and grab them. I could feel her bush scraping my tender ass. I refrained from wriggling into her embrace, leery of the consequences. She raked the length of my sides with those long, lacquered nails. Although she didn't draw blood, it hurt almost as much as if she had. I whimpered. She drew them across the length of my cock and I'm not ashamed to say I screamed.

I wondered if the patrons in the bar upstairs could hear me and whether anyone would try to rescue me. Then I realized what the name Paddles must mean. No one would react to my screams, they probably heard similar ones every night.

The snap of latex jerked me alert. I felt a cool slimy finger working its way into my bung hole and I tightened.

"If you resist me, it's going to hurt, a lot." Her voice almost sounded as if she liked that idea.

I tried to relax, but she kept working her fingers—first one, then two, then three—around inside my ass.

"I bet you're a virgin, aren't you?"

I started to reassure her that I wasn't when I realized she didn't mean my cock. "Please, Mistress, don't," I whispered.

She reached around with an ungloved hand and stroked my cock. "If you relax, you can learn to enjoy it."

I sobbed. I heard the glove pulled off, some fumbling, and the sound of buckles fastening. Then a large, hard piece of plastic, slick and cold, got shoved up my ass. I heard her breathing get heavy while she slid it in and out of my ass. I felt her come, her body pressed against mine as she shivered all over. The plastic thing didn't really hurt. In fact, when I relaxed and paid attention to her orgasm, it almost felt good. I thought about what she said and tried to enjoy it. After more thrusting, and another orgasm on her part, I decided it felt kind of nice. I actually missed it when she took it out.

She pulled up my head by my hair and kissed me again, long, slow, lingering. Afraid to kiss her back, I tentatively touched my tongue to her lips. She sucked it out of my mouth into hers. When she released me, she unfastened the clips holding my ankles and wrists to the chair, but she left the leather cuffs in place. She grabbed the ring on my collar and led me over to the table. I expected her to make me lie down, but she eased her backside up onto it without releasing my collar. She tugged my face between her legs and my cock twitched.

Damn, she tasted good. I licked and I sucked and I brought her off several times. She took my hands and placed them on her breasts and I enjoyed squeezing the dense mounds. That seemed to please her too, because she moaned when I gently pinched her nipples. My cock dripped with precum and my balls felt ready to burst. She pulled me away from her tasty twat, jumped down from the table, and patted the leather padding. I got up on there, lay down on my back, and let her clip my wrists and ankles again.

Then to my great delight, she climbed up on the table, straddled me, and lowered herself onto my cock. I moaned. God I needed to come.

"You come if and when I tell you." She moved up and down on my shaft and I had to bite my lip to keep from exploding.

I think she had come four or five more times—I stopped counting—when she said, "You've been a good boy, so I'm going to let you come tonight after all."

She slid up and down until I yelled and exploded in the most intense orgasm I have ever experienced before or since. I lay there panting, hoping she was through with me. But, she worked her way up my chest to sit on my face. "Clean up your mess, boy."

I definitely do not like the taste of my own jism, but mixed with her sweet juices I decided I could tolerate it. When I had licked every drop of it from her thighs and bush and cunt, she slid off the table and removed my restraints. She led me over to a regular wooden chair against the wall, sat down and pulled me down to my knees.

She sat in front of me in a chair and stroked my head, running her fingers through my hair. When I stopped shaking, she pulled my head back and kissed me once again. Then she attached a leash to my collar and led me over to the cage. She unlatched the door and held it open. I crawled inside and she closed the door and fastened a padlock through the latch.

The kid came down the stairs and kneeled before her. "Mistress, all the customers have left. May I lock up?"

She rummaged through the pockets of my jeans, retrieved my keys, and handed them to him. "Yes. Then wheel this boy's bike around to the garage. He's going to stay with us for a while."

"Yes, Mistress. Thank you, Mistress." The kid rose to his feet and left.

I curled up on my side and watched Mistress pull her clothes back on and disappear up the stairs. I didn't move until the kid came back with a liter bottle of water which he handed through the bars of my cage.

I just stared at him, naked now except for the collar and some sort of clear plastic device encasing his cock. The sheath attached to a ring behind his balls and a inch-wide metal padlock hung on the front of it. A small vinyl strap held a black, electronic box to his scrotum. I remembered the remote control that Mistress had activated when she wanted him to come into the bar. It had two buttons.

He left and I examined my cage. It looked homemade and didn't seem that sturdy. I guessed if I used my legs to push against the sides at the corner, I could bust it open. Problem was, I didn't want to. I grabbed the water bottle and took a long, slow swallow.

Starting Over

By I.G. Frederick

I felt like a ten-year-old who had entered a chocolate shop and found every case had a "free" label on it. When I walked into the brightly lit dungeon, I discovered two dozen naked boys, in every size from skinny to huge, kneeling in a row on the thick carpet. They ranged in age from early twenties to late fifties. I stuffed my canvass duffle into one of the cubby-holes near the entrance so I could survey the goodies.

At that moment, I finally forgave my friend Paula for co-ercing me into attending this event. Since my own pet had walked out on me four months ago, I'd stayed home from all the parties and anything else lifestyle related. I found it difficult to spend time with friends who complained about their submissives' minor misdeeds when mine had committed the ultimate transgression. It hurt to watch other women playing with their toys when I didn't have one of my own.

Here, though, any FemDom could claim one of the prof-fered toys for the evening. I recognized some of the boys who were owned by women I knew, on loan for the event. A few had no owners, and many of them I had never seen before. Some of those looked rather cute.

The large room — bigger than my entire apartment — had St. Andrews' crosses, bondage tables, cages, spanking benches, a suspension rig, and a sling. Posters on the blood red walls showed both male and female submissives in various bondage positions. Techno music played in the background.

I wore a one-piece leather corset dress that I had found at a thrift store for only twenty dollars. That, with black stockings and three-inch heels, made me feel sexier than I had in a long time. Before I could give the boy toys more than a cursory glance, Paula, Angeline, and Barbara embraced me with enthusiasm.

Angeline adjusted the bottom of her leather corset. "We're so glad to see you back in circulation."

Barbara put a latex-encased arm across my shoulders. "That boy didn't deserve you."

Of course Paula gloated. "Bet you're glad you came." She waved an arm toward the lineup. "Surely there's someone there you want to take home."

"I'll be satisfied if I have a toy to play with for the evening." I had no idea where Paula got the idea that I could find someone I wanted to collar so easily. I had spent months online and interviewing prospects before I found Richard. "I haven't had anyone to abuse in so long."

Angeline couldn't resist getting her digs in. "Perhaps if you selected someone closer to your own age, you might have more luck, long term."

I extricated myself from my friends to avoid spitting at her and greeted other FemDoms I knew. Then, I turned my attention to the boys on display. Each wore a play collar from which dangled a three-by-five tag on which they, or their owners, had written a list of "activities" in which they were willing to participate.

They all kept their eyes down and their chins on their chests, so I couldn't really see any of their faces. After months without a toy to play with, I found their equipment of more interest, anyway. I skipped over the pudgy boys, the older ones, and anyone who wasn't at least partially erect. Cock and ball torture is probably my favorite sadistic activity, but it really isn't any fun with a limp prick. And the bigger the toy, the more skin to hurt.

A well-endowed, tanned, blond youth — he looked about twenty-three — caught my eye. He had written CBT at the top of his tag in bold black letters and put the blindfold sticker at the bottom of his list. His engorged cock pointed at my feet. With a wicked grin on my face, I stepped behind the line. The blond had a gorgeous ass as well.

I knew this was one of the few opportunities I would have to play with such a luscious toy. At his age, with his looks, he could find a younger, prettier Domme, anytime he wanted. I'm pushing forty and have to use dye to keep the grey out of my red hair. While I don't exactly qualify as a BBW, I'm no size ten either. I figured, I might as well claim someone who would look good at my feet and had the equipment to keep me entertained. Then, at least when I went home alone I'd have fond memories of the evening.

By now, several of the other Dommes had walked back where the boys couldn't see us and wouldn't know who had claimed them. I tied a folded black bandana over the blond boy's eyes and clipped my leash to his collar.

"Thank you, Mistress," he whispered.

I had to take a deep breath and swallow hard to recover my equilibrium. I so missed hearing those words. *Enjoy the moment*, I told myself and patted him on the top of his head. His leash in one hand, I grabbed the duffle I keep my equipment in with the other. I led him to a table and guided him onto his back. With small, nylon pet collars and snap rings I fastened his wrists above his head and clipped them to two of the numerous eye bolts that protruded from the wooden edge of the padded table. I attached his ankles to the table so his knees faced the ceiling and his lovely, tight ass sat at the very edge, his big balls hanging down over his cheeks.

His bondage brought a smile to my lips — boys look so lovely when they're helpless and vulnerable and this one was probably the prettiest toy available at the party. I made sure the blindfold didn't bind too tightly and grabbed a fistful of his silky hair. Bringing his ear up to my mouth, I asked: "What's your name, boy?"

"Eric, Mistress."

"What's your safeword?"

"Red will work fine, Mistress. Thank you."

I let his head drop back and ran my hand down his neck to his chest. The sparse, blond bristles of hair felt so different than Richard's dense, black fur. I missed having lots of chest hair to yank on, but relished the softer feel of skin against my palms.

The boy's splendid cock still stood erect, awaiting my attention. Although shorter than Richard's, it was significantly thicker. I drew one finger down the length and it twitched in response which made me smile again. I grabbed a bag of clothes pins and let them drop out onto Eric's stomach, knowing he would guess what I intended to do with them. One by one, I clipped them to his freshly shaved ball sack until all two dozen stuck out in every direction. Each clip brought a wince to the boy's face, and a "Thank you, Mistress" to his lips, but his cock remained upright. Richard, who had a very low pain tolerance, would have started screaming by now and wouldn't have stayed completely hard. This boy certainly seemed more fun to play with.

With another wicked grin, I ran my hand across the ends of the clothespins. His twisted grimace sent me looking in my bag for the metal "finger massagers" that I had purchased at a health food store. They look like springs soldered in a circle and I rolled one down the length of Eric's cock. He moaned. The thickness of his dick expanded the massagers much more than Richard's thin rod had. I imagined the metal pinched more. I placed a second massager around the shaft just under his cock head, watching to make sure it didn't constrict blood flow.

I had acquired my next implement from a kitchen outlet. After the dot-com bust a few years back, my employment situation suffered. Without much of a toy budget, I learned to find creative options in pet shops, hardware stores, and discount kitchen shops. When Richard left, he took most of the nicer toys he had bought me, so I was back to pervertibles. Designed for cutting pastry, the device I extracted from my bag has a metal wheel with a fluted edge. Not quite as painful as a Wartenberg wheel, but still quite effective, especially on a cock's sensitive skin. Licking my lips, I rolled it up and down the length of Eric's hard prick.

He moaned again and lifted his hips a little into my movement. I liked his reaction — much more enjoyable than Richard's pleas for me to stop — so I leaned over and kissed him. He responded hungrily, tasting my lips with his tongue. I had finally, after months of effort, taught Richard how to kiss sensuously. Despite being the same age, Eric didn't need any lessons.

When I got bored with the pastry wheel, I reached for a hair clip that had plastic nodules inside. I put that around Eric's cock between the massagers — the teeth couldn't quite close — engendering another moan. I leaned over, allowing my long hair to brush across Eric's chest so he would think I planned to kiss him again. This time I bit his nipple, hard. He squeaked. I bit the other one, pressing my teeth into his flesh until he yelped. I couldn't help chuckling — pain tastes so good.

With one hand holding his cock up by the back of the clip, I flogged the exposed flesh with a small wire whisk, occasionally letting the metal strike his stomach or reaching over to hit his inner thighs. He wriggled his hips, but didn't make a sound. His skin reddened and my clit twitched.

I grabbed his hair again and whispered in his ear. "How're you doing, boy?"

"Fine, Mistress, thank you. You have unusual toys. I like them."

I laughed. Richard said my laugh had a wicked resonance that would shame Dorothy's nemesis. I watched Eric shiver at the sound, although I couldn't tell if fear or delight caused his reaction. I leaned over and pressed my teeth into the head of his cock until he screamed.

By now, I had pussy juice dripping down my thighs and I desperately needed some relief. I checked Eric's tag, then fumbled in my bag for a bottle of lube and my purple, vee-shaped, double-sided dildo. Pulling off my soaked thong, I slipped the egg-shaped knob of the shorter end inside my cunt, suppressing a gasp of delight. I slathered lube on the other, longer end that now protruded from my pubic hair. When I inserted gloved, lube-slick fingers inside the boy, he sucked in his breath and moaned. I panted with desire and need.

I slid the shaft into his sweet ass, the ribs at the base of the dildo where the two ends met rubbed against my clit, and I shuddered with orgasm. The boy sighed with obvious pleasure. Although he stole all the rest of my toys, Richard left my dildo behind. I assumed he did so because he hated taking it in the ass. I had derived some of my enjoyment from forcing him to accept something he disliked so much. But now I found myself relishing the big smile plastered across Eric's face. I slid in and out of him until I brought myself off again. I felt so good after that, I leaned over between his legs and planted a kiss on the top of his cock. It twitched and he moaned again. I had to wonder what it would feel like to sit on a rod that thick.

While I rested for a moment and enjoyed the aftershock spasms in my pussy, the surrounding activity penetrated my attention. Leather floggers whizzed through the air striking the skin of boys bound to crosses. A boy in a cage, with his ankles and legs trussed up behind his back, squealed as two women poked at him with bamboo canes. A woman in a black lace body stocking hit the bright red ass in front of her with a wooden paddle. Her boy, who was bent over one of the spanking benches, yelped and screeched.

Paula had bound her boy in the sling and penetrated him with a strapped-on dildo that made mine look minuscule. Barbara lay face down on a table with one boy massaging her back and another rubbing her feet. When she saw me looking her way, she winked at me. I couldn't see Angeline anywhere and guessed that she had taken her boy into one of the half dozen smaller, private rooms.

Steadying myself on my feet, I slid the dildo out of Eric's ass and my cunt, dropped it into a plastic bag, and trashed the gloves. Then, I lifted Eric's soft blond hair away from the sheen of perspiration on his face. "You still game, boy?" Richard would have begged me to stop twenty minutes ago and I wondered if Eric hadn't had anyone play with him in a long time. Shame if a boy this pretty couldn't find an owner. But maybe he was just a pain slut, not interested in submitting beyond the bedroom or the party.

"Perhaps Mistress would care to try some of the other activities listed on my tag?" His voice had a tight edge to it and I admired him for not safe-wording me. I kissed him again, this time thrusting my tongue deep into his mouth and letting it dance with his.

When I removed the hair clip, he whimpered. Each clothespin came off with a sob and my pussy got wetter. I rolled the finger massagers off his cock, slowly to maximize the pain, and he groaned.

"Thank you, Mistress," he whispered. I stroked the soft, now-naked flesh. "You have lovely fingers."

I wrapped those "lovely fingers" around his shaft and squeezed until he groaned again. Then I ran a hand across his muscular chest. *I wish I could take this one home*, I thought to myself. Maybe, like Richard, he appreciated an older Mistress.

After gathering up my toys, I unclipped the collars

around his wrists and ankles from the eyebolts on the table, and watched amused as the boy struggled, while still blind-folded, to clean off the padding with a wipe I had found in a canister on one of the tables set around the room. Then, I led him by the leash over to an empty spanking bench. *No reason not to enjoy playing with this toy as long as I can.*

Eric kneeled on the bench and bent his chest over the pad-ded top. I clipped his arms to eyebolts near the base and he let his head hang down, ready to take whatever I chose to inflict on him. I caressed his fine, tight ass with my hand, reveling in the firmness. Alternating between a leather belt Richard had left behind and a wooden spoon, I walloped Eric's backside until it had a nice, red glow and the ache in my pussy had be-come unbearable. I unclipped the boy's wrists, stuffed every-thing in my duffle, and led him by the leash over to one of the sofas along the far wall. Paula sat at one end, her boy kneeling in front of her, kissing her feet and sucking on her toes. She gave me an intoxicated smile. I settled on the other end and pulled on the leash until my boy lowered himself to his knees. I grabbed his hair to tilt his head back and kissed him.

I wanted to push his face between my legs, but he hadn't put oral worship on his tag so I pulled the bandana blindfold off his face and leaned back. The boy gave me a long, linger-ing glance, taking in tits pushed up and waist pinched small by the corset. Although he didn't raise his eyes to my face, I could see him checking out my pale skin and green eyes through his long blond lashes.

To my surprise, a smile brightened his face and he leaned over to kiss my hand. "If I may say so, Mistress is quite beau-tiful. I hope she isn't done playing with me, yet."

"Hardly," I laughed, giddy at the thought that this beauti-ful boy found me attractive. I looped one leg around the back of his neck and urged him forward, hoping the missing activ-ity was just an oversight. He didn't require more prompting than that, lifting my skirt and kissing his way up the inside of my thigh. I settled back into the cushions while he licked the juices off my pubic hair and then worked his tongue inside my slit. A moan escaped me when he slid it across my clit and it didn't take long for him to bring me off.

That didn't slow him down. "Mistress tastes so very good." He lapped up the extra juices and sucked and licked until I came again and again. I had to give the boy credit for perceptiveness. He quickly figured out what I liked best and the orgasms became more and more intense until I had to take a break.

I pulled his hair, dragging his head out from under my skirt and bringing him up on the sofa next to me. Kissing him, I tasted myself on his full lips. I stroked his silky hair with one hand, slid my other down his back, and allowed him to slip his arms around my waist. It felt so good to have a boy in my arms again, even if only for the evening. That, combined with the glow from countless orgasms, made me wish the boy were available..

Releasing his lips, I guided his head onto my shoulder. We sat there for a long bit, while I played with his hair and ran my hand along his back. But, instead of asking directly about his ownership status, I put the ball in his court. "Tell me about yourself, boy."

"Not much to tell, really." He shifted his head so his lips touched my neck and his hot breath tickled my skin. "I'm a computer programmer. I own a small house on the northeast side and I'm building a dungeon in the basement. I've had four or five years' lifestyle experience. What else would Mistress like to know?"

May as well go for broke. "Do you have an owner? Are you looking for one?"

"I regret to say I've never found a woman I wanted to belong to who thought me worthy of her collar. I would very much like to." He reached out with his tongue and, without moving his head, licked the length of my neck. That and his words sent a shiver down my spine. "May I ask if Mistress is in the market for a pet?"

I managed to suppress a gasp and respond with more calmness than I felt. "As a matter of fact, I am." I ran my fingers through his hair. "But, I need more than just a play toy."

"I'm very obedient, Ma'am. I've had training as both a houseboy and a sex toy." He slipped out of my arms, onto his knees, and lay his head on my thigh. "I earn a nice living, I've tried to create a home that a woman would enjoy living in, and I make a very presentable escort in vanilla circumstances. I don't smoke or do drugs, and I only drink alcohol in moderation."

I patted the top of his head, trying to maintain my composure. "You certainly seem to have all the qualities I would want in a pet. Of course, a long-term relationship requires compatibility and chemistry as well."

"If Mistress will permit me to say so," he pushed my skirt back far enough to kiss the inside of my knees, "at least on my part, the chemistry is quite strong. I hope, since Mistress chose this boy to play with, she finds his appearance acceptable."

I laughed. I couldn't believe this boy would consider giving himself to me after one encounter, but I had never met a boy I wanted to own so much. "More than acceptable." I grabbed his hair, pulled his head back, and kissed him. "You're downright adorable."

When I released him, he said, "Thank you, Mistress. May I ask, have you ever owned a slave?"

I bit my lip to keep back the tears and waited until I could speak without my voice shaking. "I collared a boy a year and a half ago. He left me four months back. Like so many, he claimed to want complete control, but then tried to top from the bottom and complained about my restrictions."

"Mistress, I can assure you that should you ever find me worthy of your collar, I would never presume to question your authority or give you anything less than my total devotion. But, the truth is it's just as difficult to find a woman willing to take complete control of a man. I don't want to be someone's partner, I want to be her slave."

I closed my eyes and wondered if I could ever put my collar around another boy's neck. Richard's desertion had devastated me. Still, I knew I didn't want to live alone. And this boy seemed to have everything I could possibly want: he learned fast, seemed to understand the owner/slave dynamic, had a nice build, tolerated lots of pain, and knew what to do with his tongue. But what did he see in me?

I heard a door open across the room and saw Angeline step out leading a boy on a leash, following her on all fours. She had a glazed look in her eyes. I stood up and tugged on my own leash. The boy grabbed my duffle and I took him into the small room furnished only with a bed that had eye hooks along the top and bottom rails. Whatever came of this night, I wanted to enjoy everything this boy had to offer.

I locked the door and waited while Eric put clean sheets on the bed from the stack on the wooden shelf above the headboard. When he turned around to face me, I pushed on his chest until he sat down. Throwing one leg over his, I straddled his thighs and pulled him against my breast. I ran my fingers through his hair, kissed him then guided his mouth down my neck to my tits. He covered them in kisses, licking and caressing them with his lips. I could have purred. Richard was a leg and foot man and had to be reminded to give my jugs the attention they craved. When Eric finally lifted one tit reverently from my corset so he could wrap his lips around my nipple, I almost came from the delicious sensation it sent to my clit.

When I couldn't bear the tension any longer, I shoved him back on the bed and guided him into a position where I could clip his wrists to the top rail. At that point, I didn't have the patience to worry about securing his ankles. I crawled up over his shoulders and sat on his face, dripping my juices all over him. With his tongue flicking everywhere I wanted it, I came three times before I eased myself down over his chest and stuffed his cock up inside me.

Damn, he feels good there. I discovered thick had definite advantages over long. I rode Eric for nearly twenty minutes, until I could see a drop of blood where he bit into his lip. "You may come now, boy."

His blue eyes twinkled with relief and excitement. "Thank you so much, Mistress." Didn't take the boy more than three strokes to finish off with a grunt and I wondered how long he could have held out. Richard would have begged for permission long before now.

When Eric stopped spurting, I unclipped his wrists and rolled over on my back next to him. "Clean up your mess, boy."

"Yes, Mistress; thank you Mistress." He crawled toward the foot of the bed and lapped and sucked all his jism from my bush and my cunt, bringing me off another couple of times in the process.

I grabbed his hair and pulled him up so he could lay with his head on my shoulder. I stroked the skin of his muscular arms and back while I floated in post-orgasmic euphoria. For the first time, I rejoiced in Richard's departure. Barbara was right, that fool didn't deserve me. "Well, boy, if your house-keeping skills prove as good as your abilities as a sex toy, I might just have to collar you."

"Oh, Mistress, thank you. Nothing would make me happier than to be owned by such a beautiful and Dominant woman. I just know you could truly take complete ownership of me." He lifted his head enough to kiss the shoulder that had cradled it. I grabbed his hair and pulled his lips to mine.

The Cougar and the College Boys

By I. G Frederick

"Sorry to leave you here all on your own," Lenore tossed clothing into a worn, red leather suitcase. "But, with Chris in the hospital and Suzanne out of the country, I'm the only one who can manage the office." She zipped up the bag and pulled it off the bed. "I know I promised you time away from it all, I just didn't mean for you ..."

Tess shook her head. "Don't worry, hun. Accidents happen. I'll be fine, really. You have lots of books and, well, I've got some thinking to do."

Lenore dropped her bag and gave Tess a hug, enveloping her in the scent of lavender. "You *sure* you're going to be okay all by yourself?"

"Don't worry about me. I'm getting used to being alone. At least here there aren't any memories." Lenore had bought

47

the cabin only a year before Kevin and Tess had finally parted ways and they had pretty much stopped socializing as a couple by then.

Lenore held Tess at arm's length for a moment, looking for a chink in her armor. She shook her head. "There's plenty of food *and* wine. The store will deliver if you give them 24 hours notice, and ..."

Tess patted Lenore's arm. "I'll be fine. I can bike into town if I need to and from what I've seen of your pantry, there's enough food here to last me a month. Go, you don't want to miss your plane, you've got at least a two-hour drive."

Lenore looked at her watch. "Crap." She hugged Tess again. "I'll only be gone a week, two tops. Suzanne's due back on the sixth." Grabbing her suitcase, purse, and car keys, she hurried out the door.

Tess watched the dust cloud disappear into the trees from the cabin's wrap around porch. When the roar of the car's engine faded in the distance, she let the silence envelop her. She shivered, not sure about staying out in the middle of nowhere by herself. But, she hadn't wanted to give Lenore any more worries — her friend already had a cancelled vacation and a boss laid up with a broken leg and dislocated shoulder to contend with.

Crossing her arms under her breasts, Tess gripped her biceps until the sense of abandonment dissipated. She had to remind herself that Kevin, not Lenore, had abandoned her and when she recovered from his betrayal she probably would be better off. She closed her eyes and inhaled the scent of pine trees and listened to the gurgle of the brook tumbling over rocks behind the cabin. Tilting her head, she judged that she probably had several more hours of daylight. She went inside long enough to grab a key and a hat, locked the front door, and set out along the path that followed the stream.

Most of the cabins were empty — owners usually only came up on weekends until June. But, she noticed an Explorer and a Jeep parked outside an A-frame on the opposite bank. As she approached the trestle bridge that carried the road over the brook, three men in their early twenties emerged from the A-frame and collected an aluminum pony keg, a large cardboard box with chip bags protruding from the top, and a huge blue cooler with wheels from the back of the Explorer.

"Someone's planning to party," she muttered to herself. At least the cabin was far enough away from Lenore's that the noise shouldn't invade her solitude. And, it was nice to know if she did encounter some kind of emergency, there were vehicles nearby. Tess passed the bridge and found the narrow dirt path that would take her through the trees to Lenore's cabin.

Once back inside, she flipped on the light and put the kettle on. While she waited for the water to boil, she perused the built-in bookshelf that extended the length of one wall of the cabin. Reaching to the ceiling, it was filled with hardbound copies of every best seller published in the last decade. Tess fixed herself a cup of jasmine tea and settled down with a copy of Mark Twain's autobiography.

When a series of knocks rattled the front door an hour later, Tess jumped and dropped the book. She tried to remember if she'd locked the door. Approaching cautiously, she noted the deadbolt was turned, but the transom above the solid oak was tilted inward. Listening, she heard nothing from the porch. She flipped on the light, rose up on her tiptoes, and looked through the peephole. The blond who had hefted the keg onto his shoulder as if it weighed no more than the potato chips stood on the porch, holding his empty hands out slightly from his side, palms facing her. She hesitated, then slid the chain into place before flipping the deadbolt back and cracking the door.

"Sorry to bother you, but yours seems to be the only occupied cabin within a mile of ours, Richard forgot the matches, none of us smoke, and we've no way to light our campfire," he blurted out. "Of course, we didn't figure this out until an hour after the only store in 20 miles closed for the night. I don't suppose you've any spare matches. Or a lighter?" He looked forlorn and adorable at the same time.

"Hang on, I'll check." Tess closed the door and threw the deadbolt back before looking in the pantry. She found a full package of boxed matches and, unbolting the door, handed two through.

"Thank you SO much. You're a real party saver. I don't suppose you'd like to come join us? We've a keg of porter, we're going to roast wieners once we get the fire going, and we've got marshmallows for S'mores."

"It's just you fellows?"

"Yeah, but we're harmless. I promise. We all just graduated from University of Portland. This is our last week together before we go our separate ways." He grinned, dimples forming in his cheeks, his blue eyes sparkling. "Having you there would keep us from getting rowdy. Besides, you're a darn site easier on the eyes than my roomies."

Tess couldn't help smiling back. "Thanks for the invite, but it sounds like you fellows have a history — I'd just be an intruding stranger."

"Ladies are never an intrusion, especially one as lovely as yourself." He put one hand in front and one hand behind his waist and bowed. "Don't say no. Why don't you think on it? Feel free to wander over anytime."

"Sure. Have fun, regardless." Tess pushed the door closed and turned the bolt. She found her place in the book, but it no longer held her interest. The temperature had dropped and she shivered. She stared at the empty fireplace, but couldn't find the motivation to move logs from the basket to the grate. Wandering into the kitchen, she pulled out a can of soup, but forgot where Lenore kept the opener. For some reason, she had a yen for hot dogs. She wondered if they had yellow mustard or if they'd brought something better.

"Don't be ridiculous, they're half your age." Tess rummaged through the kitchen drawers until she found the can opener, but then paused with the blades resting on the lid. "It would be a good way to get your mind off Kevin." But, would watching untouchable young hard bodies guzzle beer ease the ache of climbing into an empty bed every night?

Tess tossed the can opener back in the drawer, wrapped herself in a fleece jacket, grabbed a flashlight and her key, and stomped out of the cabin. She hesitated, turning the key back and forth. Finally, she drew it out with the bolt locked and followed the path toward the A-frame. The glow of their campfire lit up the yard outside the cabin and Tess turned off the flashlight to watch. Four young men sat in camp chairs around the fire talking. Not exactly a rowdy bunch. She flicked the light back on and made her way to the bridge.

When Tess entered the light of the campfire, the blond jumped up. "Fabulous. So glad you decided to join us." He pushed his chair toward her. "I'm James." He pointed to a dark skinned young man with kinky hair. "Peter."

A tall fellow with shoulder-length brown hair jumped up and bowed. "I'm Richard." The fourth, rose to his feet and towered over the rest of them. "Gerald. And, you're...?"

"Tess." A wave of male pheromones washed over her and she wondered if she'd made a mistake.

James proffered his hand and when she reached out, he lifted her fingers to his lips. "Pleased to make your acquaintance."

Each of them kissed her hand in turn. Tess relaxed and sat in the camp chair. Peter handed her a plastic cup full of dark brown liquid.

"What would you like on your dog?" Richard asked. "We've got relish, kraut, mustard, and onions."

"What kind of mustard?" Tess took a sip enjoying the delicious smoky malt smell and the complex flavor of hops.

"Beaver, of course. We stuck with local as much as we could. None of us're staying in Portland." He sounded wistful. "Horseradish or honey?"

Tess smiled. "Horseradish mustard and relish, please."

"Chips?"

She looked at the table where half a dozen open bags of different kinds of Kettle chips were spread out next to packages of graham crackers, bags of marshmallows, and a pile of chocolate bars.

"I wouldn't mind a few barbecue flavored chips, thanks."

Richard poured chips from the bag onto the plate. The chair had a cup holder, so she put her beer there to free both hands to take it from him. She watched the four fill their own plates and wondered if they'd been waiting for her or decided to have seconds. The "dog" was still hot, slightly blackened on the outside, juicy at the center. She'd never known anyone to consider bratwurst in sourdough buns "wieners," but she was soon engrossed in the bite of the horseradish contrasting with the sweet relish, both enhancing the spices and fat in the sausage.

Someone handed her a paper napkin just as a bit of juice trickled down her chin and she looked up to see Gerald smiling down at her. He dropped to a squat. "James was right, said you were hot. Why's such a pretty lady hiding up here in the woods alone?"

Tess's pulse skipped a beat and she clenched her jaw, mentally measuring how far she would have to run to get to the bridge.

"Good grief, Gerald, you're going to scare her away." Peter scooted his chair closer to hers. "Don't mind Sasquatch here, four years of college couldn't civilize 'im." He shrugged. "We only keep him around for hoops."

"Seriously," Richard stood in front of her and held the barbecue chip bag over her plate. "After we got here we just realized we missed feminine company more than we'd expected. When we saw you walking on the other side..."

James punched him in the shoulder. "Matches."

Tess laughed. They may have had more in mind than sharing their dinner, but she no longer felt threatened. They were all good looking and muscular in their tight purple tee shirts. She wondered what would happen to their camaraderie if she decided to take one back to Lenore's cabin. She handed Richard her empty plate. "Thanks, but I'm saving room for S'mores." She wiped grease and relish juice off her fingers with the napkin and opened her coat. The campfire's heat had chased the evening chill away. She shrugged her jacket off, letting it hang over the back of her chair.

Three wolf whistles caused her hands to fly to cover the low cut neckline of her form-fitting cotton top.

"Guys," James scolded. "You promised."

"We're sorry," Peter and Richard chorused together. Gerald was still staring at her figure.

"I guess all that gym time paid off." Tess had hidden from Kevin and her disintegrating marriage at the health club, often spending a couple of hours a day rotating between the aerobic equipment, circuit training, and pools.

"Most certainly." James' look had the same fire as those of his buddies.

Tess smiled, but realized it wouldn't be right to bring a strange man to Lenore's cabin and she doubted three would want to stay outside while she took one of them into their A-frame. But she hadn't had sex for, she had to stop and count, eighteen months. And they were all so gorgeous.

"The Lady asked for S'mores.." James pulled away and set out plates. Peter jumped up and laid out the graham crackers while Robert and Gerald opened chocolate bars. James handed each man a fork, keeping two for himself, and bowed to Tess, presenting her with the marshmallow bag. "Shall we compete for your," he cleared his throat, "confections?"

She laughed, pulled the bag open, and pierced two white treats on each fork. "I like mine barely toasted on the outside and gooey inside."

Peter bowed. "May the best roaster win." The four turned their forks toward the fire, carefully keeping them out of the flames. Minutes later, they each knelt before her offering plates of perfectly toasted marshmallows, the chocolate under them already melting. On second glance, she noted that Gerald's had just a teensy bit more brown than she liked and Richard's had flattened even without the top graham cracker. She reached for that one.

"They all look wonderful, but this one seems perfect." She rewarded him with a smile. "Thank you, Richard."

The crestfallen looks on the others' faces resolved Tess' dilemma. "I like mine with double chocolate, though. James could you get me another bar? And, I think this is going to get messy, perhaps Peter, you could get me some more napkins. Gerald, I could use a bit more beer." She really didn't need to drink anymore, but she wanted to let them know she wasn't favoring one over the other.

They scrambled to fill her requests, then stared while she lifted the gooey sandwich to her lips and sighed with pleasure as the sticky combination melted on her tongue. They'd even had sense enough to purchase dark Moonstruck chocolate instead of the more commonly used, and less satisfactory, Pennsylvania option. She closed her eyes and savored the flavor combination.

"Perfect." She licked her lips.

"Yay," Richard shouted.

Gerald mashed the top of his graham cracker onto his marshmallows so hard that all the white seeped out and he scooped it up with his fingers. The others consumed theirs with a bit more grace. Tess dragged her tongue the length of her sticky index finger. Two empty plates dropped to the ground, Gerald clutched his to his chest, and James crushed his. The fire popped and crackled while she sucked her finger into her mouth and the four gasped in unison.

This is just too easy. Of course, even though they'd only been in the woods a few hours, they'd probably been immersed in finals studies for weeks, which to a young man must seem like months if not years. She pulled her finger out with a pop and ran her tongue across first her top and then her bottom lip. Their breathing got heavier. She lowered her eyes to scan for bulges and was not disappointed.

"I hope you don't think I'm presumptuous, Tess." James voice had sunk a full octave. "But, could you let us know who you've picked? You're driving us all crazy."

Tess tilted her head and looked at him. "Why do I have to choose?"

They all gasped again.

James inched closer, wiping the sticky off his hands on his denim shorts.

She stared into his baby blues. "I'm not nearly as picky about men as I am about marshmallows, and I appreciate variety."

Peter scooted his chair closer to hers. "All of us?" His dark eyes had widened to silver dollar size.

She bit her upper lip, giving herself a second to change her mind. "Why not? You do have condoms?"

Three of them looked horrified, but Richard sprinted for the Jeep. "I do!" he shouted over his shoulder. He returned to the group moments later with a box of a dozen, still shrink wrapped, and a huge tube of scented lube.

Peter kissed the inside of her wrist. James leaned forward and licked a graham cracker crumb from just above the neckline of her shirt.

Her heart raced and her breathing grew heavy. "I assume there's a bed inside?"

Richard scooped her up into his arms and headed for the A-frame before she realized what he was doing.

"Wait."

He stopped, but didn't put her down.

"I meant with blankets ... you could bring out ... to cover the ground. If you keep the fire going ..."

Gerald ran inside and returned with his arms full of quilts and blankets. James and Peter each tossed another log on the fire then helped Gerald spread the blankets out in front of it. Richard eased down and deposited her gently. The heat of the flames washed over her, but it didn't compare to the warmth spreading from within. Peter and Richard knelt on either side of her and took her hands. One by one, Richard sucked each finger into his mouth, tantalizing her with his tongue. Peter kissed her pulse, then inched his tongue along the inside of her arm toward her elbow. Gerald sat cross legged at her feet and fumbled with the laces of her boots. James knelt at her head, leaned over and kissed her forehead.

Tess melted into the heat of male lips caressing her skin, setting her on fire. When he finally managed to pull off her socks, Gerald sucked on her toes. James had worked his way down to her neck and without removing her fingers from his mouth, Richard fumbled with the button on her jeans. Tess pushed his hands out of the way and undid them. Her jeans and panties slid down her hips and disappeared. James helped her sit up and pulled her top over her head while Peter unhooked her bra and Richard pulled it away. She heard four sharp intakes of breath as her tits fell out of the lace restraining them.

Peter and Richard lunged towards her, but then each gently lifted a breast to his lips. Peter teased her nipple with his tongue and Richard sucked adoringly at the other. Just before her eyes rolled back into her head, Tess noticed he had the most blissful expression on his face and she wondered if any of them were virgins. U of P was a Catholic school.

Gerald licked his way up her legs and Tess' hips lifted in response. Her skin burned with passion, the flames centering between her legs. Gerald's heat disappeared and she opened her eyes to see him tossed aside by James who dove between her legs and planted soft, blazing kisses on the tops of her thighs, her bush, her lips. Tess closed her eyes again and moaned. Richard and Peter continued lathering her breasts with their tongues, Gerald went back to sucking on her toes, and James buried his tongue into her slit.

She pushed her hips into his face, willing him to find her clit. His lips clamped around it and she exploded in his face.

He chuckled, the vibrations teasing her further, and suckled her nub until she came again. This time when she opened her eyes, Tess realized she was surrounded by naked male bodies, their skin glistening in the firelight, their hard cocks pointing at her. James licked her juices off his lips and the tip of his nose, giving her a wide grin.

"Condoms?" she managed to whisper.

Someone presented her with the opened box and she pulled out four with the same color wrapping. Tearing the corner off one, she shuffled them in her hand and presented them fanned out, the torn corner hidden beneath her thumb. "Who wants to go first?"

Peter and Richard grabbed for condoms and looked crest-fallen when the packets they selected were whole. James took one of the last two and bowed to Gerald when his also emerged intact. Gerald's eyes widened to fill half his face and his hand trembled as he reached for the remaining packet. Tess smiled at him, but he just averted his eyes. *The group's virgin?*

He fumbled with the packet and the rubber, his hands shaking. Tess was afraid to touch him, worried she'd terrify him. Despite his nervousness, his cock still jutted out in her direction, the swollen glans dripping precum that sparkled when it caught the fire's light.

When he finally got himself sheathed, Tess reached up. "Come here big boy. You're in for a treat."

He knelt between her legs, his green eyes dark with lust and fear. She reached up both hands and he lowered his body over her. She pulled his face toward hers with one hand behind his neck and reached down to guide his cock into her with the other. Although she opened her mouth, he pressed his lips together. Then his cockhead pushed into her cunt and he gasped. His eyes looked as if they would burst from his face before he closed them. Moaning, he eased himself deep into her folds.

Tess moved her hands to his round, firm ass, squeezing

when she wanted him to pull out and pushing down to get him back inside. They'd barely gotten the rhythm established when he shouted "Oh. My. God." and lay still in her arms.

He picked up his head and seemed almost in tears. "Tess. Miss. I'm so sorry."

She kissed him. "It's okay. I'm guessing that was your first time. And, you don't have to worry about leaving me hanging — I'm sure your roomies will pick up the slack."

Gerald started to pull out and she grabbed him around the waist. "Hold onto the condom so it doesn't spill." He did as she requested and crawled over to the far corner of the blanket.

"Do you care which of us goes next?" James knelt by her side, running one hand softly up her leg, across her tummy to her breast.

"Any more virgins?"

James shook his head, licking his nose, reminding her what he had done to her clit with his tongue.

"Triple play?" Tess had never been with more than one man at a time and she had three gorgeous cocks presenting arms. Why not take them all at once?

"If that's your pleasure."

"Any of you experienced in anal?"

James reached for the lube. "I am." He grinned, sheathed his cock, and looked at her.

Tess tilted her head. Of the other two, Richard had the larger cock. She struggled to her knees, pointed to him, then patted the blanket in front of her. He rolled on a condom and lay on his back. She straddled his legs and turned to look at James. He nodded and she mounted Richard holding still while James splurted lube on his fingers. He rubbed some on his cock and slid first one coated finger and then a second into her ass.

He knelt behind her and caressed her ass with his dry hand. "Ready?"

She nodded, her cunt full of cock, bracing herself on her hands and knees. James worked his way in slowly, then slid in and out while Richard bucked his hips. Tess looked up at Peter and licked her lips. He sunk to his knees in front of her, his cock just out of reach. She formed an O with her mouth and he slid in, his balls barely clearing Richard's face. She moaned, unable to move, filled with delicious cock from every angle. The three gradually matched each other's rhythm so James pushed into her from behind as Peter plunged his cock deep into her mouth and Richard thrust his hips upward grinding his pubic bone against her swollen clit. They all pulled away then rammed back into her.

Peter's smooth cock caressed her tongue, filling her mouth with the taste of musk and eucalyptus and Richard and James massaged her G-Spot between them. Richard held her hips and James reached around her to squeeze her breasts. Unable to moan or call out, Tess whimpered, overwhelmed by the onslaught of fabulous sensations. The shaking started in her wrists which threatened to give way. She locked her elbows and the trembling moved from her breasts to her cunt until she spasmed from the inside out.

They moved faster and a chorus of grunts and moans emerged from their throats. Tess was still coming when one by one they exploded. She collapsed on Richard's chests until James eased out of her then slid down to her side, one breast flopped across Richard's chest, the other pressed into his side. Someone stretched out behind her, hard chest against her back, semi-rigid cock resting against her crack. The heat of male bodies combined with the glow from the campfire enveloped her.

She guessed that Gerald had rejoined the group, because she felt lips on her toes. Fingers ran through her hair and she lifted her head. A leg slid underneath to make a hairy pillow. Drifting somewhere between euphoria and sleep, she realized they wanted more. The cock against her ass was rigid and another one was pushing against her forehead. Tess tried to shake her head, but she was barely able to move it. "Can't … do … more … tonight. Tomorrow?"

"Of course." James' voice was still husky. "You just let us know when." The back of someone's fingers caressed her cheek. "You want us to take you back to your cabin?"

"Please."

Gerald carried her wrapped in one of the blankets from the A-frame. Someone extracted the key from her jeans and she sank into the sofa when he set her there.

"I'm leaving my cell number on the table in case you need us." James' breath caressed her cheek. "Just come by whenever you'd like or I can send Gerald if you don't feel like walking."

Tess managed a blissed out smile. Being single certainly had some advantages. She heard the door close, the bolt turn, and the key bounce on the floor after it dropped through the transom. "Tomorrow," she whispered.

Acknowledgements

This book would not have reached your hands without the help of many dear friends and colleagues. I thank my readers and supporters, especially Cindy, my proofreader, editor, and best friend. Thanks also to all those who have served me, well and ill, over the years. I have learned something from each one of you and I hope that you find what you seek.

Other fiction
by I.G. Frederick includes:

Complicated Couplings
Four sexy stories about tangled twosomes

"If You Love Someone" — Tara leaves her husband to move in with Nathan, but he abandons her after a few months. When he returns, begging her to take him back, life and love look very different.

"Commiserate" — The same man dumped them both. When they commiserate, they discover more in common than an ex-boyfriend.

"Passion's Price" — Richard steals Gina's heart from three thousand miles away. But, when he moves across the country, her intensity and passion for life drive him away.

"Lunchtime Lover" — Both married, they started their affair with the promise never to fall in love. Then Lisa's divorce becomes final.

www.eroticawriter.net/ComplicatedCouplings.html

Dommemoir

In Geneviéve's journey of discovery she dabbles in the BDSM lifestyle which forces her to recognize and acknowledge her true nature. Her memoir, woven together with that of a male slave, draws the reader into an intense odyssey of sexual expression triumphing *over sexual repression while delivering fascinating insight about a different kind of love.*

"The aptly titled Dommemoir *delivers on so many levels... It quickly sucks you in and envelopes you in the bondage of its spell...* Dommemoir *is a character study ... placing you in the delicious bondage of its dark and compelling landscape..."*
Larry Brooks, USA Today bestselling author

WARNING:
This book changes women's attitudes about relationship dynamics, forever.

www.eroticawriter.net/Dommemoir.html

Eleanor & Mick
A journey of sexual exploration and insight
In five sizzling hot stories, Eleanor seeks refuge in a small town on the Oregon Coast and befriends her younger neighbor. He captures first her heart and then her submission, taking her on a journey of sexual exploration and insight.

"Salt for His Wounds" — When Eleanor's ex-husband shows up begging for a second chance, she asks her young, gorgeous next door neighbor for a favor and Mick takes advantage of the opportunity.

"The Mercantile" — Eleanor attributes Mick's detachment to the difference in their ages, but Mick confesses a need for kink. Afraid of losing him, Eleanor reluctantly consents to bondage and pain.

"The Things We Do for Love" — When her gorgeous girl-friend visits Eleanor on the coast, Mick's obvious attraction troubles her. But, Liz only has eyes for Eleanor.

"Paid in Full" — Mick's army buddy finds Eleanor hot and makes a deal with Mick. But, if Mick really loved Eleanor would he let another man have sex with her?

"Renovations" — After Mick spends a month renovating their garage, Eleanor discovers he built in a few surprises.

www.eroticawriter.net/EleanorMick.html

Family Dynamics

Six sultry stories exploring sexuality in Dominant/submissive liaisons

"'Aunt' Grace" — Jen needed a place to stay in Portland and turned to her father's stepsister. But, she found so much more than she ever dreamed possible with her *"Aunt" Grace. Second Place, NLA:I Short Story Award.*

"Leather Family" — Kyle needs his own boy. Jacques would do almost anything to find a place in a Leather Family. But, Kyle serves a female Master.

"Searching" — Two dominants love each other, but need someone who submits to them both. Just how far will young Jeremy go to serve the lovely Lady Theresa?

"Taking Control" — To free the woman she loves from a horrid sadist's perverted games, Melanie must set aside her own aversion to men.

"Family Ties" — When her slave's ex faces eviction,

Katherine offers refuge. But can Naomi pay the price?

"Said the Unicorn" — Tessa dedicates herself to her Master's service, so his determination to add another woman to their family devastates her.

www.eroticawriter.net/FamilyDynamics.html

Fork In The Road

Changing people's lives, and relationships
in three pairs of sexy stories

"Said the Unicorn" — Tessa dedicates herself to her Master's service, so his determination to add another woman to their family devastates her.

"Proposals" — The evening appears perfectly arranged for him to pop the question. But, Christopher's proposition takes Geraldine on an unanticipated sexual adventure.

"Winners & Losers" — When he finally walks away from the blackjack table, Jeffrey finds someone worth gambling on.

www.eroticawriter.net/ForkinRoad.html

Ladies in Love
Six sizzling stories of Lesbian Lust

"Empty Seat" — Laura offers Alex a nightcap as thanks for help with a presentation to a prospective client. But they never order drinks.

"'Aunt' Grace" — Jen needed a place to stay in Portland and turned to her father's stepsister. But, she found so much more than she ever dreamed possible with her "Aunt" Grace. Second Place, NLA:I Short Story Award.

"Spa Date" — Dismayed that she introduced Sam to the woman who betrayed her, Julie tries to fix her up again.

"Taking Control" — To free the woman she loves from a horrid sadist's perverted games, Melanie must set aside her own aversion to men.

"Dental School" — How can Cindy flirt with the beautiful blonde dental instructor while her mother propositions the student examining her teeth on Cindy's behalf?

"Commiserate" — The same man dumped them both. When they commiserate, they discover more in common than an ex-boyfriend.

www.eroticawriter.net/LadiesinLove.html

Lessons Learned
Sometimes you need more than love

Four sizzling hot FemDom love stories about women who come to terms with their dominant sides and discover that *makes them more attractive to the men they love.*

"Tea Party" — What if the first time your best friend drags you to a FemDom "Tea Party" you see your former boyfriend serving canapes naked?

"Blind Date" — How do you respond when you find your ex-husband hanging out at the restaurant where you planned to meet your "Blind Date"?

"To Serve" — If you love a vanilla woman and you only want "To Serve," how do you introduce her to the lifestyle without scaring her away?

"Change in View" — What if a "Change in View" alters the attitude of the man you mentored so he could find his perfect Mistress?

www.eroticawriter.net/LessonsLearned.html

ℒove ℋurts
but in a good way
Five steamy stories about the dark side of love

"B&D Trainee" —Online, Xavier promised to make his B&D fantasies come true. But, had he jumped in over his head?

"Knife Play" — Seeking a knife he saw online, Jack inadvertently found himself in a room full of pain and bondage contraptions. He almost turned around and left, but a beautiful woman taught him a different way to appreciate blades.

"Pussy Whipped" — Eric knew nothing about BDSM, but purchased a ticket to a fundraiser to help out his friends. When Miranda asks him to "play," he discovers exactly what those four letters mean.

"The Auction" — He attended the auction with only one goal — to acquire a very special whip. But an offer to try it out proved irresistible and he discovered sometimes events, and women, can exceed one's expectations.

"FemDom Fairy Tale" — A FemDom's offhand remark about a photograph at an erotic art show draws a handsome man's attention. But, when two dominants find each other attractive, which one chooses to kneel?

www.eroticawriter.net/LoveHurts.html

Second Chances

Six sexy stories about getting a second shot at the gold ring

"Back to School" — An admin error forces Jordan and Dennis to share a dorm room. Older than their classmates, they decide to stick together. But Jordan's past threatens to keep them apart.

"Gordon" — When the cover model of her latest book walks into the coffee shop where she writes, Lenore embarrassingly calls him by her character's name. His reaction confounds her.

"Spa Date" — Dismayed that she introduced Sam to the woman who betrayed her, Julie tries to fix her up again.

"Salt for His Wounds" — When Eleanor's ex-husband

shows up begging for a second chance, she asks her young, gorgeous next door neighbor for a favor. Mick takes advantage of the opportunity.

"Proposal — Tangled Webs" — The evening appears perfectly arranged for him to pop the question. But, Christopher's proposition takes Geraldine on an unanticipated sexual adventure.

"Starting Over" — When her pet walked out on her, she stayed away from parties because it hurt to watch other women playing with their toys. But, a friend coerces her into attending a unique event.

www.eroticawriter.net/SecondChances.html

When Two's Not Enough
Seven sexy ménage stories

"Tribal Fusion" — Whenever and wherever he dances, Dominic collects propositions, but the Lady Lenore's proposal takes him by surprise.

"Two Brothers" — A divorcée in a flashy sports car attracts the attention of two young virgin brothers visiting the "big" city of Boise.

"Honeymoon" — Although she expected to honeymoon aboard a cruise ship, Allison finds herself sailing on a private yacht staffed by an incredibly beautiful couple. Believing her new husband wants to hide his older, less attractive wife, makes it difficult to en-

joy the hedonistic delights offered in paradise.

"Jail Bait" — Serena wants Joshua to pop her cherry, but he won't touch her because of her age. When her birthday finally makes it legal, he arranges for a very special celebration.

"Nikki's Birthday" — Even someone happy in a monogamous relationship might find the gift of a hot, new toy for an evening of decadence incredibly exciting. (Inspired by a real birthday present given to a lovely little bi-sexual, genderqueer slave.)

"Market Boy" — When a beautiful Domme offers Jack the opportunity to serve at a party for her friends, he responds too quickly and too eagerly, getting more than he bargained for.

"The Cougar and the College Boys" — Alone in the woods, hours from Portland, Tess discovers four college friends staying in a nearby cabin. The boys invite her to share their campfire, their dinner, and ...

www.eroticawriter.net/TwoNotEnough.html

Young & Eager
Barely legal but hardly innocent

"Two Brothers" — A divorcée in a flashy sports car attracts the attention of two young virgin brothers visiting the "big" city of Boise.

"Teachers Pet" — *Trapped at an all-girls' school in the middle of nowhere, Sabrina tries to get her hunky teacher to bust her cherry.*

"Arresting Development" — *Bethany went out with Officer Rick to avoid a speeding ticket, but discovered she enjoyed getting "arrested."*

"Jail Bait" — *Serena wants Joshua to pop her cherry, but he won't touch her because of her age. When her birthday finally makes it legal, he arranges for a very special celebration.*

www.eroticawriter.net/YoungEager.html

Or visit
http://eroticawriter.net/
to find links to individual stories
and additional collections
and

For darker, edgier fiction
look for books by
KORIN DUSHAYL
The Darker Side
of Intimacy
transgressivewriter.com

www.ingramcontent.com/pod-product-compliance
Lightning Source LLC
Chambersburg PA
CBHW061451170626
46811CB00004B/1462